THE ARABIAN NIGHTS

CHILDREN'S COLLECTION

Dados Internacionais de Catalogação na Publicação (CIP) de acordo com ISBD

J76p   Jones, Kellie
        Prince Camar and Princess Badoura / adaptado por Kellie Jones. - Jandira : W. Books, 2025
        136 p. ; 12,8cm x 19,8cm. - (The Arabian nights)

        ISBN: 978-65-5294-180-0

        1. Literatura infantojuvenil. 2. Contos. 3. Contos de Fadas. 4. Literatura Infantil.
        5. Clássicos. 6. Mágica. 7. Histórias. I. Título. II. Série.

2025-597   CDD 028.5
                                                                                                          CDU 82-93

Elaborado por Vagner Rodolfo da Silva - CRB-8/9410
Índice para catálogo sistemático:
1. Literatura infantojuvenil 028.5
2. Literatura infantojuvenil 82-93

The Arabian Nights 10 Book Collection
Text © Sweet Cherry Publishing Limited, 2023
Inside illustrations © Sweet Cherry Publishing Limited, 2023
Cover illustrations © Sweet Cherry Publishing Limited, 2023

Text based on translations of the original folk tale,
adapted by Kellie Jones
Illustrations by Sarah Grace

© 2025 edition:
Ciranda Cultural Editora e Distribuidora Ltda.

1st edition in 2025
www.cirandacultural.com.br
No part of this publication may be reproduced, stored in a retrieval
system, or transmitted in any form or by any means, electronic,
mechanical, photocopying, recording, or otherwise, without written
permission of the publisher.
This book is a work of fiction. Names, characters, places, and incidents
are either the product of the author's imagination or are used fictitiously,
and any resemblance to actual persons, living or dead, business
establishments, events, or locales is entirely coincidental.

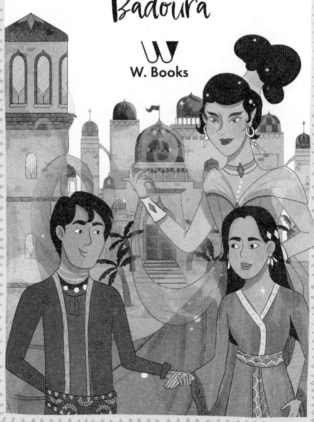

Long ago, in the ancient lands of Arabia, there lived a brave woman called Scheherazade. When the country's sultan went mad, Scheherazade used her cleverness and creativity to save many lives – including her own. She did this over a thousand and one nights, by telling the sultan stories of adventure, danger and enchantment.

This is just one of them …

King Shah Zaman
The King of the Isle of the Children of Khaledan

Prince Camar
The son of Shah Zaman

The Grand-Vizier
Shah Zaman's friend and advisor

Maimoune & Danhasch
Two genies who cannot agree

The Gardener
An elderly man

Princess Badoura
The Princess of China

The Emperor
Badoura's father

King Armanos
The King of the Black Isles

Princess Hayat
The Princess of the Black Isles

Marzavan
Badoura's childhood friend

Chapter 1

Many years ago, some twenty days' sail from the coast of Persia, there was an island known as the Isle of the Children of Khaledan. Nature had blessed it with more fields than desert and as many animals as trees. Mankind had only added to the beauty by building an exquisite palace with flowers that spilled

Persia
An ancient empire in southwestern Asia, now called Iran.

from each balcony, and holy places that shone with mosaic in the sun.

The king of this island was called Shah Zaman, and he knew

himself to be one of the luckiest and most peaceful kings on earth. The only thing fortune had not given him was a son, and he and his wife had almost given up hope.

Shah Zaman shared this sadness with his friend, the grand-vizier, who advised him: 'Since this is a matter

grand-vizier
Someone like a modern-day prime minister. They did not just advise royal families in the old Turkish empire and in Islamic countries, they represented them and led the government. More powerful than a vizier.

only Allah can help with, Your Majesty, you should spend even more time in prayer, and continue to live a good life in service of your people. Allah may yet give you a son in return.'

So Shah Zaman did not give up. He doubled his efforts to be the best king he could be and prayed that nature would take its course. He was rewarded a year later when the queen gave birth to a son. They named him Camar al-Zaman, meaning 'Moon of the Century'.

Allah
The Arabic word for God, used in the Muslim religion.

As the long-awaited son of such a successful king, Prince Camar grew up with the best of everything, including the best teachers. His father loved him so much that he could have easily become spoilt and horrible, but Camar grew up to be charming and clever. He was still a teenager when his father began to think about making him the next king. The grand-vizier advised against it.

'The prince is still too young,' he said, 'for such a responsibility.

Let him marry first. Give him a family to run, and then you can begin teaching him how to run a kingdom.'

'I can always rely on you to give good advice,' the king praised him. 'Very well, I will begin looking for a wife for Camar.'

When the prince heard of this, however, he was not pleased.

'Father, forgive me, until now I have always done as you asked,' he said. 'But this time I cannot. I am too young to marry.'

It was the first time the prince had ever said no to his father. It was

not what the king had expected, but he tried to reassure Camar by saying: 'It will take some time to find a suitable bride, Camar. You will be older by the time we do.'

'But not necessarily any wiser, father. There is still much I do not know about the world beyond this palace. Everything I know is from books and study.'

When the king repeated this to the grand-vizier, his advice was: 'Then give the prince some real-world experience, Your Majesty.'

Shah Zaman nodded. 'I know just the thing!'

From then on, Camar was part of the king's council. These were the people who advised the king about matters involving the kingdom, its closest neighbours and the politics and trade between them. This was not what the young prince had wanted,

nor what the grand-vizier had meant by "real-world experience". What Camar wanted was to go out and see the world with his own two eyes. But the king was too protective. He never let Camar out of his sight
for fear that something might happen to him.

'Well, my son,' he said after a year of work on the council. 'Now that you are older – and I hope wiser – are you ready to marry?'

'No, father.' The prince was just as firm as before – *firmer*, even. It was not just that he had spent the past year studying maps, realising just how big the world was and how he had seen none of it. He also could not stand the idea of marrying a woman he did not love.

'Camar still refuses to marry,' Shah Zaman told his grand-vizier. 'I have never known him to be so stubborn about anything.'

'Then you must be just as patient,' the grand-vizier advised. 'Why not give the prince another year? If you revisit the idea of marriage again in front of the whole council, he will not be able to refuse you.'

Shah Zaman agreed, but he was so upset by the delay that he spoke to his wife, Queen Fatima.

'If Camar will not listen to me,' he said, 'then perhaps he will listen to you. You must make him understand that he will be

punished if he continues to disobey me after another year.'

He sounded so serious that the queen immediately spoke to her son.

'Why are you being so stubborn?' she asked.

'Is it stubborn to want to choose my own wife?' Camar replied. 'And not just because she is a princess, but because she is someone whose character suits mine?'

The queen bit her lip. Secretly she agreed with her son, but all she could say was: 'Your father will punish you if you do not marry in a year.'

The prince shrugged. 'Marrying the wrong person would be a punishment anyway.'

Despite this reply, Shah Zaman introduced his son to several princesses from neighbouring kingdoms over the next year. Camar was polite but completely uninterested in any of them.

At the end of the year, he was called before his father and the council. The king repeated his wish for Camar to marry. Camar repeated his refusal. As punishment, he was taken to an old tower and locked away at the top of it.

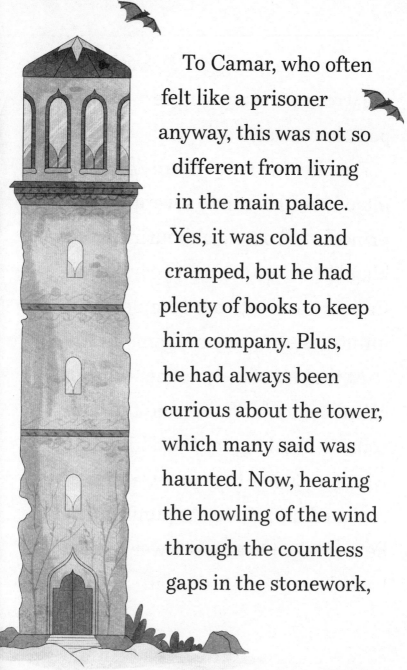

To Camar, who often felt like a prisoner anyway, this was not so different from living in the main palace. Yes, it was cold and cramped, but he had plenty of books to keep him company. Plus, he had always been curious about the tower, which many said was haunted. Now, hearing the howling of the wind through the countless gaps in the stonework, he thought he knew the cause of such a rumour. But he was wrong.

The truth was that those rumours were because of a genie called Maimoune who liked to visit the tower. In fact she thought of it as her own since it was always empty, only now, of course, it was not.

One night when the prince was asleep, Maimoune flew up to the topmost room of the tower and saw Camar in his bed.

What a beautiful boy! she thought. *I wonder what he did to be locked away like this?*

The question sent her imagination racing and she stayed some time just to watch him sleep, and to play with the lock of hair that fell across his forehead. Finally, she kissed his cheek and continued her flight around the kingdom. She overheard several people talking about the prince who would not marry, and the king's punishment.

Maimoune soon met another genie called Danhasch, who had dark wings and a darker character. While Maimoune liked to help humans, Danhasch liked to play tricks on them. He did this by spoiling fresh milk, stealing left socks and occasionally making someone cluck like a chicken in front of those they really wanted to impress.

'Danhasch!' shouted Maimoune the moment she saw the other genie flying through the air. 'What are you up to?'

'Nothing at all, mighty Maimoune,' Danhasch lied. Maimoune was much more powerful than he was, and he did not want to anger her. 'I am just returned from China, one of the largest and most powerful kingdoms in the world.'

'Not as large and powerful as Persia,' said Maimoune. Aside from being competitive, she always liked to support whoever

and whatever Danhasch did not.
She would have said that an
orange was blue and the earth
was flat rather than agree with
him on *anything*. Danhasch was
exactly the same but would never
admit it.

He ignored Maimoune and
continued: 'I have been watching
over the most beautiful princess
I have ever seen.'

'What a coincidence,' said
Maimoune, 'for I have been
watching over the most beautiful
prince I have ever seen. He is
asleep in my tower.'

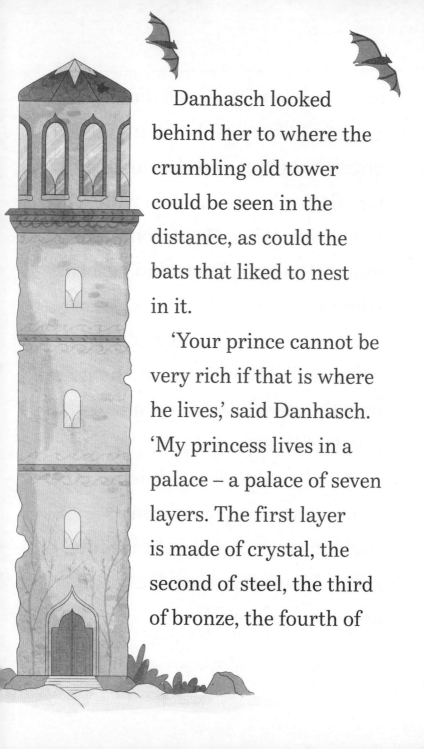

Danhasch looked behind her to where the crumbling old tower could be seen in the distance, as could the bats that liked to nest in it.

'Your prince cannot be very rich if that is where he lives,' said Danhasch. 'My princess lives in a palace – a palace of seven layers. The first layer is made of crystal, the second of steel, the third of bronze, the fourth of copper, the fifth of silver, the sixth of pure gold and the seventh of a special kind of marble that looks like trapped rainbows.'

Maimoune refused to be impressed. 'My prince has been cruelly imprisoned by his father and yet suffers in silence. Those who can survive hardship bravely are far more interesting than those who are always spoilt and happy.'

'"Happy"?' Danhasch barked. 'My princess is not *happy*! Her father, the emperor, built that palace to protect her from all the

---

emperor
The male ruler of an empire.

suitors who came for her hand in marriage. When she declared that she was so comfortable there that she never wanted to marry at all, he locked her up in it!'

'Oh, to be locked away in a palace must be terrible indeed,' said Maimoune sarcastically.

'Come and see for yourself,' said Danhasch. 'You will see that no one can beat my princess for beauty or suffering or ...' he paused to remember what else they were arguing over. 'Or ... *interestingness*,' he added awkwardly.

---

suitor
Someone who wants to marry someone specific.

'Hah! Why should I go all the way to China to prove you wrong when we only need to go *there*.' She pointed with a clawed hand to the tower. 'I will show you my prince and you will see that he is the most beautiful, the most interesting and ...' she paused, 'the most ... *sufferingest*.'

But when at last they were both inside the tower and hovering over the sleeping prince, Danhasch would admit no such thing. Secretly he thought that the prince and the princess looked quite similar, from their clear skin, perfect features and shiny black hair. Openly he said, 'But you see, half my princess's great beauty is in her incredible eyes. I cannot see your prince's eyes at all. And how am I to judge who is more interesting while one is asleep?'

Maimoune frowned, seeing a flaw in her own plan. 'And how will *I* know that you are even telling the truth if you say that she is in any way better than he is?'

After more arguing, during which they said the same thing in different ways, they 'agreed' to bring the Princess of China to the tower. With a flash of magic this was done, and a sleeping princess was laid down beside the sleeping prince. Then the two genies could look upon them both at the same time.

'Her eyes are closed too,' Maimoune observed. It was better than admitting that the princess was indeed just as beautiful as the prince. 'And she has drool on her cheek.'

'At least she is not snoring,' Danhasch said, looking pointedly at the prince.

Since each genie felt that their human was the most beautiful, they decided to summon a third to break the tie. Maimoune stamped her foot to summon Caschcasch. A hideous, hump-backed genie with six horns seemed to sprout through the floor.

'Caschcasch,' said Maimoune, 'which of these humans is the most beautiful?'

Caschcasch looked at the prince and princess with admiration but could not choose a winner. 'Why not wake them one at a time?' he suggested. 'Then you can see who is more impressed by the other.'

'An excellent idea,' said
Danhasch. 'We should hide or
they will be too busy looking at us
to look at each other.' With that,
he transformed into a mosquito.
Maimoune, of course, transformed
into a bigger mosquito. But neither
was a sensible choice given the
number of cobwebs in the room.
Caschcasch simply disappeared the
same way he had come.

Outside the tower, from across
the horizon, the sun was rising, but
to speed things along, Maimoune
the mosquito stung the prince's
neck. Then she buzzed away

before he could swat her. Camar opened his eyes, which Danhasch saw but did not say were very beautiful. They grew huge and round when Camar took in the sleeping woman next to him. Far from being impressed by her loveliness, however, he was annoyed. He shook the princess awake.

'Did my father send you?' he demanded the second her eyes were open.

The princess's response was to scream and jump up on the bed. 'Where am I?' she cried, looking around her at the bare stone walls and simple furniture.

But no answers came because neither royal could understand the other. In a flash of magic, Maimoune made it so that the prince spoke Chinese. Not to be outdone, Danhasch made it so that the princess spoke Persian. Both asked the same question in their new languages:

'WHO ARE YOU?'

Chapter 2

The prince and princess scowled at each other, he from beside the bed and her from on top of it.

'Who am *I*?' Camar said. 'As if you do not know! The only way you can be here is if my father brought you. And if he thinks I will change my mind about marriage because of a couple of chilly nights in a tower, he is sadly mistaken.'

At the word "tower", the princess ran to a window and looked down down *down* to the ground far below. She took in the unfamiliar landscape beginning to glow with dawn light. 'Where am I?' she repeated. Next, she ran to the wooden door and yanked at the handle. It did not open. 'Let me out!'

'We are locked in together. But you already know that.'

Camar spoke with folded arms and a stern face. But as he watched the princess pound on the locked door until her fists grew red, he realised that she was genuinely upset. Even frightened.

'Stop!' he said. 'You are hurting yourself. The guards cannot hear you, but I promise you are safe.'

Then he moved as far across the room as he could – which was not far – to give her space. 'Please, sit down.'

There was only one chair and the princess took it. She was breathing hard. 'Last night,' she said, 'I went to sleep in my own room. How can I have woken up here?'

'I have no idea,' the prince replied. 'But my father must have had something to do with it. He is desperate for me to marry.'

'Mine too. He locked me up when I refused.'

'Mine too!'

They surprised themselves by smiling at each other, each realising for the first time how beautiful the other person was.

Camar cleared his throat and crossed the room. 'Let me see your hand,' he said. One of the princess's knuckles was bleeding from where she had split it on the door. 'You should take your ring off,' he suggested. 'Just in case your fingers swell up.'

The princess nodded and slid the ring off her slender hand.

'Beautiful,' Camar remarked. Adding quickly: 'The ring, I mean.'

'It was my mother's,' the princess said. She took Camar's hand and slid the tiny ring onto his little finger. 'You can look after it for me.'

The prince laughed and took off his own ring. 'This was my father's, and you can keep it for all I care.'

'Is he that bad?

'He never used to be.'

'Mine neither.'

Camar's ring was so big that the princess had to put it on her thumb. She fiddled with it while Camar dabbed the knuckles of her other hand with a cloth.

'You have a lot of books,' she observed, looking around the tiny room. 'Do you like to read?'

'Yes. Books are how I see the world.'

'Me too. Which one is your favourite?'

Camar showed her. Showing her led to reading to her, and eventually they took it in turns reading the male and female voices of the story. They were having so much fun that the morning passed by more happily than any they could remember. Then the princess's stomach rumbled.

'Do they not feed you?' she wondered.

'Ah,' Camar said. 'That may be my fault. I threw my food out of the window yesterday – in protest, you understand. I expect my father told the guards not to bother giving me any today. All I have is …' he reached for a half-empty bowl beside his bed, '… two, four, six, *seven* olives.'

'I love olives!'

They ate three olives each.

Camar hid the seventh behind his back and asked the princess to choose a hand. When she chose wrongly, he gave her the extra olive anyway. The princess threw it high into the air and caught it in her mouth. Camar clapped.

'My father should have introduced you to me sooner,' said Camar.

'Why?'

'Because I never would have said no.'

They smiled warmly at each other. Afterwards they talked and read some more, and the prince helped the princess to brush her long black hair. This last activity was so relaxing that they fell asleep side by side on the bed. They were still smiling.

The two mosquitoes that were Maimoune and Danhasch took

to the air and returned to their genie forms.

'Who do you think was more impressed by the other?' asked Maimoune, looking down at the sleeping humans.

'It is clear that your prince found my princess very beautiful,' replied Danhasch.

'Just as it is clear that your princess found my prince very interesting.'

'And since they have both been locked up by their fathers for the exact same reason, their suffering is equal.'

Mentally, Maimoune added up the score. 'A tie, then?' she asked.

'More like a draw,' Danhasch corrected her. 'Now I will take the princess home …'

When Camar woke the next morning, the first thing he did was turn to the princess. She was not there. His heart sank. Luckily a guard soon appeared with some breakfast, and even though his belly was growling with hunger, the first thing Camar did was ask where the princess was.

The guard looked puzzled. 'What princess, Your Highness?'

'The princess from yesterday.'

'You have had no visitors, Your Highness.'

'She was here all day, I tell you!'

This went on, back and forth, for some time. Eventually the prince grew angry and the guard grew worried. He fetched the grand-vizier who entered the tower room to find Camar pacing impatiently.

'Your Highness,' the grand-vizier greeted him, 'how are you today?'

'You will be glad to know that I am ready to follow my father's wishes,' said the prince.

'Oh?'

'Yes, as long as she agrees to it, I will marry the princess who was here yesterday.'

The grand-vizier wore the same puzzled look as the guard. 'But Your Highness, there was no princess.'

'On the contrary there was the most wonderful princess I have ever imagined.'

'Are you sure you were not dreaming, Your Highness?'

'Yes, I am sure! Now go and tell my father that he will have his way.'

The grand-vizier was so troubled

that he did indeed go straight to the king, only to tell him that he feared the young prince had gone mad.

'Mad?' the king repeated. 'What do you mean?'

'I mean that he is raving about a princess who was in his room yesterday. He says he will marry her as you wish. But the guard confirms that the door has been locked and no one has come or gone for days.'

The king immediately followed the grand-vizier to the tower to see his son.

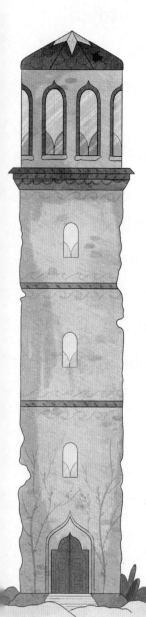

'Camar,' he said. 'What is this nonsense about a princess?'

By now the prince was getting cross. 'What is nonsense, father, is you continuing to punish me after I have finally agreed to get married. *You win!* Now please just bring her to me.'

'What is her name?' the king asked.

'Her name …?' Camar faltered. 'I do not know …' Of all they had said and shared with each other, names had not seemed important. Until now.

'Where is she from?' the king asked next.

'I do not know exactly, but she has her own palace. Her father locked her up in it because she refused to marry.'

'I see …' the king shared a glance with his grand-vizier. 'And what does she look like?'

'Beautiful!' Camar gushed. 'She is about my height, with black hair and brown eyes, and she *loves* to read–'

'Camar, you are describing

yourself! It was a *dream*, son.'

Angrily, Camar waved his hand in his father's face. 'Is this a dream too?' He was talking about the delicate ring still on his little finger. 'This is hers!'

The king was surprised, having never seen the ring before. Then Camar ran to the little table and waved a stained cloth. 'This is her blood from where she hurt herself banging on the door!' Then he grabbed his comb and pulled out a hair that was far longer than all the others.

'This is her hair!'

This evidence was enough for the king.

'I believe you,' he said, 'but whoever she is, she was not brought here by me. Together we must try to find her.'

With that, Camar left the tower for good. He and his father searched the whole island for the princess, and elsewhere in Persia, not knowing that she lived in China. As time passed, Camar's hope of finding her grew weaker and weaker. Finally, it died altogether.

For the princess, whose name was Badoura, the situation was even worse. Despite the ring she still wore on her thumb, no one believed that the prince she spoke of was real. When she awoke and told her father that she was ready to marry the man of his choosing, he thought she had gone mad. 'Which man?' he asked.

'The one you sent me to yesterday!' she cried. 'Surely there cannot be that many. Where is he?'

There was a flush to her cheeks and a brightness to her eyes that the emperor had never seen before. Mistaking love for a fever, he immediately summoned a nurse.

'Her body is healthy,' the nurse reassured him, 'but her mind is not. She keeps talking about a prince in a tower. I am afraid there is nothing more I can do for her, Your Majesty.'

So the emperor began looking for someone else who could cure his daughter. Many healers tried. All failed. And it was impossible to hide what was happening from Badoura.

'You think I am making him up!' she cried. 'I am not! His father locked him away because he will not marry!'

The emperor blamed himself for her madness, and rather than upset her further, he told all the healers who came next that if they failed to cure her too, they would be executed. After that, there were no more healers, and Badoura refused to see her father.

Her only visitor was her childhood friend Marzavan, who had recently returned from his travels and heard all about the princess's supposed madness.

executed
Historically, when someone was killed as a punishment by law.

'My prince is real, Marzavan,' Badoura swore. 'And you would love him too if you met him. He is so funny and kind.'

'I believe you,' he said. 'But I have travelled all over China and I have never heard of a prince in a tower.'

'Maybe it was not in China,' she said.

'Then how could you understand each other?'

'I do not know! But is that any stranger than how I came to be there in the first place? How I managed to leave my palace and enter his without anyone –

including me – knowing? I do not care about any of that. I just want to find him.'

'Can you describe where you were?' asked Marzavan. 'Did you see anything outside the tower?'

The princess nodded. 'The rooftops there were different.

Smooth rather than tiled. I can remember domes and archways.'

'And the prince's clothes?'

Badoura blushed. 'He was wearing his sleep clothes.'

'It is not much information to go on, but I promise that I will look for him when I go travelling again.'

'When will that be?'

'Soon,' he promised.

Marzavan kept his word. The moment he left China, he went from city to city, country to country, and kept his ears open for gossip and rumour. After four months, he reached a large town with a busy port called Torf. There he heard a great deal about Prince Camar al-Zaman, whom some said was mad and others said was lovesick. He sounded so much like Badoura that Marzavan immediately set sail for the Isle of the Children of Khaledan where the prince lived.

The prince, Marzavan soon learnt, never left the palace alone. But one day he saw the grand-

port
A town or city with direct access to water, where ships can load and unload passengers and goods.

vizier go into an apothecary and so he followed him. Inside the shop, the older man squinted at the writing on a medicine bottle, unable to read it.

'Allow me,' Marzavan offered, and read the label for him. The grand-vizier put the bottle back. 'What is it you are looking for?' Marzavan asked. 'Perhaps I can find it for you.'

The grand-vizier sighed. 'I do not think what I am looking for even exists. Can you heal a broken

apothecary
Someone who sells or prepares medicines, now called a pharmacist. Also the name of the place where medicines are sold or prepared, now called a pharmacy.

heart? How do you help a young man who has given up on life?'

'You talk to him?' Marzavan suggested.

'I have tried that.'

'Then perhaps someone his own age should talk to him?'

The grand-vizier looked more closely at Marzavan, noting that he was about the same age as Camar. He wore strange clothes and spoke their language with an accent, but he was clearly well off and well educated.

He must have come from far away, the grand-vizier thought.

If nothing else, he can talk to the prince about his travels. Perhaps that will distract him from the missing princess ...

At last, the grand-vizier nodded. 'Come with me,' he said.

Chapter 3

It was mid-afternoon but Camar was still in bed when his door opened and the grand-vizier came in with Marzavan.

'Your Highness?' the grand-vizier called into the shadowy room. 'I have brought you a visitor.'

'Unless it is a princess who can appear inside locked towers,' the prince mumbled, 'I am not interested.'

The grand-vizier sighed and left them alone.

Marzavan approached the bed. 'I do not know a princess with such magical powers, Your Highness. But I do know one who sends you a gift.'

Still not looking at his visitor, the prince raised a hand from the covers. Marzavan placed something small and heavy on his palm. The second Camar's fingers closed around it, he shot upright in bed.

'My ring!' he cried. He turned, finally looking in Marzavan's direction.

'Heavens!' said Marzavan. 'You look just like her!'

'Like who?' Camar seized his arms urgently. 'Tell me her name!'

'Princess Badoura.'

'Badoura …' Camar repeated the name of his beloved. 'Where is she? *How* is she?'

'Heartbroken, like you. And more of a prisoner than ever with her father believing that she has gone mad.'

'Not for long,' Camar vowed. 'Take me to her at once!'

The prince was standing now, casting about for clothes he had not bothered wearing in weeks.

'She is all the way in China, Your Highness. And from what I hear you are not even allowed out of the palace.'

'True,' Camar said, but he would not be discouraged. 'We will need a plan …'

King Shah Zaman was delighted by the change that suddenly came over his son. There was no more moping in bed, mourning the lost princess. Camar was up and dressed early each morning, and he could often be found studying maps the way he had done in the past. When he was not doing that, he was walking in the palace grounds with Marzavan, deep in discussion.

One day he went to his father and asked if he and Marzavan could go hunting. The king agreed because the fresh air and exercise would do Camar good. But he was only allowed to stay away for one night, and he would have six guards with him.

mourning
The feeling and expression of great sadness that follows a death or loss.

Camar and Marzavan rode their horses hard the first day, trying to get as far from the palace as they could. That night they made camp and waited until the guards were asleep. Then they ran away.

'Wait,' Marzavan hissed at the last minute, eyeing the blood from the animal they had hunted that day. 'Give me your coat.'

'Why?' Camar hissed back, although he was already taking it off.

'Your father needs to think you are dead,' Marzavan said.

'Otherwise he will keep looking for you.'

Camar hesitated for only a moment, imagining how sad his father would be if he thought that Camar had died. But then he imagined how happy the king would be when he returned, married and alive. He nodded and handed over the coat.

Marzavan smeared the coat with blood and dropped it in the middle of the forest. That way it would look like they had snuck off hunting alone and been killed by a wild animal. Afterwards, they set off for China. The journey took months, but the gossip when they arrived was the same as when Marzavan had left: the princess was still mad and no one wanted to risk death by trying to cure her. No one, that is, except Camar.

With Marzavan's help, the prince disguised himself as a travelling healer and went to the palace to offer his services. Everyone tried to change his mind, including the emperor.

'You understand,' he said, 'that if you fail to heal my daughter, you will die?'

Camar nodded. 'But what do I get if I succeed?'

'What do you want?'

'Your daughter's hand in marriage.'

'Very well,' said the emperor. 'Good luck.'

But the only luck Camar needed was in getting past the princess's nurse. Badoura had told her not to let anyone into her palace.

'I am sorry,' the woman told Camar. 'My mistress will not see anyone, even the emperor.'

'Then will you take her a letter from me?'

The nurse waited while Camar scribbled a message on a piece of paper and folded it around a small object. Then she took it to the princess. As Badoura unfolded it, a small, shiny object pinged to the floor and rolled between her slippered feet. She picked it up in a daze.

'My ring,' she breathed. And then she was running through six layers of her palace, until she reached the seventh where Camar was framed by a crystal doorway. Badoura threw herself into his waiting arms.

'So many people said you were a dream that I began to believe them!' she cried.

'If you are dreaming,' laughed Camar, 'then so am I. And I never want to wake up.'

The happy couple were brought before the emperor, who was shocked by the change that had come over his daughter. But Camar would not accept his thanks for curing her.

'She was never ill, Your Majesty. She was telling the truth. My name is Camar al-Zaman, and somehow your daughter appeared in my home.'

'Then disappeared,' Badoura added.

'But not before I had fallen head over heels in love with her.'

'And I with him.' They beamed at each other. 'If you want to thank someone, father, you should thank Marzavan. He found Camar and told him who and where I was.'

'I promise Marzavan will be richly rewarded,' said the emperor. 'And the two of you will be married.'

So it was. The whole country celebrated the 'recovery' and the wedding of their beloved princess, but none more than Marzavan.

He gave Badoura a special gift. It was a talisman carved from a reddish stone called carnelian.

'Keep it with you,' he said. 'It will bring you happiness.'

Badoura hugged him. 'You have already done that, Marzavan. Thank you.'

---

talisman
An object, often worn or carried, that is believed to protect the owner or have special powers.

The newlyweds spent the first months of their lives together in China. Then one night Camar had a dream that his father was dying. He awoke with a gasp. All his guilt over running away and pretending to be dead returned.

'What is the matter, my love?' Badoura asked.

'I must go home,' he said. 'I fear my father is ill.'

The emperor did not want to let them go. He agreed only on the condition that they return if they met any danger on the journey.

This time the journey took even longer, for Camar was travelling with many more people, including several guards on horseback and the princess and her maids in a wagon. After weeks of travel, the weather became unbearably hot. They set up camp on a huge meadow to enjoy the shade under some big trees.

Camar went inside the tent he shared with Badoura and found her taking a nap. The sash she wore tied around her waist had been laid aside, and for the first time Camar noticed the talisman from Marzavan that she tucked underneath it. He stepped outside to study it in the sunlight.

It must be very precious, he thought, *if Badoura carries it with her like this.*

Just then a large brown bird swooped down and snatched the talisman in its beak.

'Hey!' Camar cried, giving chase. 'Give that back!'

He followed the bird to the edge of the meadow where it had settled, but as soon as he reached it, the bird took flight again. And again. Camar kept following until he saw the bird swallow the talisman. At which point it took flight yet again.

Then Camar looked around and realised that he had run further from camp than he had thought and the sun was setting. Not only had he lost his wife's precious talisman; he was lost himself!

For days the prince wandered, trying to find his way back to the meadow. But every path looked the same and led first in circles, then to a seaside town.

After living off of what food he could find, Camar did not think twice before helping himself to fruit from a garden. The olives reminded him of Badoura, whom

he missed terribly. What did she think had happened to him? That he had run away and left her?
Worse?

'Thief!' shouted an elderly voice. 'Thief!' The owner of the garden came hobbling towards

Camar with a walking stick. 'Those are my olives!'

'I am so sorry,' said Camar. 'I was so tired and hungry that I forgot my manners.' And he gave such a deep bow that the old gardener immediately forgave him.

'You look tired and hungry,' he said. 'Come inside and rest.'

In exchange for food and water, Camar shared his story. 'It has been eleven days since I left my Badoura,' he concluded. 'She must have continued on to the Isle of the Children of Khaledan by now, and I still do not know how to get back there. How far away am I?'

'Hmm,' said the gardener, stroking his white beard thoughtfully. 'It is almost a year's journey by land.'

Camar groaned. *A year?*

'But,' the gardener added, 'luckily for you, there is a boat that goes from here that is much faster.'

'Excellent!' cried Camar. 'When does the next boat leave?'

'In six months. You just missed one.'

Camar groaned again. What would he do for six months? But the old gardener had already thought of that.

'You can stay here with me, if you like. I would be grateful for the company.'

'Gladly!' said Camar.

But rather than just keeping the old gardener company, Camar was determined to be useful. The first

thing he did was make a scarecrow to keep the birds off the plants.

It worked on every bird but one, which was a familiar brown bird with a hooked beak.

'You!' Camar growled. 'This is all your fault!' And he took a bow and arrow and shot the bird out of the sky.

With time the bird turned to feather and bone, and Camar found Badoura's talisman where its belly had been.

That night he put the carved red stone under his pillow and thought of his wife.

'What is Badoura doing right now?' he wondered, just before he fell asleep.

When Badoura had awoken to find her husband missing, panic struck her. *How can he just disappear*

without a trace? she thought. *The guards will take me straight back to my father if they find out. And he might never let me leave again!*

'I do not know what happened to Camar,' she told her maids. 'Or how it connects to my missing talisman. But I know that Camar will continue on to his homeland to see his father if he can. That is where we must go too. To fool the guards, one of you must pretend to be me, and I will pretend to be him.'

Luckily, Badoura was tall for a woman, and she looked enough like her husband that she could pass as him by wearing his clothes and pulling a bit of hair over her eyes. She had never ridden a horse like a man before, but she found that she enjoyed it far more than riding in the bumpy wagon. The hardest part was giving orders in her husband's voice, but the guards had always found Camar's accent strange anyway. And thanks to the genie who had brought her to Camar in the first place, Badoura could still speak Persian. When they finally reached the sea, she used Persian to hire a boat to take them to the Black Isles. This was a step closer to the Isle of the Children of Khaledan.

The King of the Black Isles, at this time, was called Armanos. He was old friends with King Shah Zaman. When he heard that Prince Camar was in his capital city, he invited him to stay at the palace. For Princess Badoura, in disguise, it was very awkward.

'You are too kind,' she said, deepening her voice

as much as possible and bowing like a man to the king and his daughter.

'Not at all,' King Armanos insisted. 'Your father wrote to me a couple of years ago inviting me to visit, but I have been too sick. The least I can do now is look after his only son. Do you remember my daughter? You have not seen each other since you were children.'

'Oh, yes,' said Badoura as Camar. 'Princess ... um ...'

'Hayat al-Nefous,' the princess reminded him.

'Princess Hayat, yes. How lovely to meet you. Again.'

This was the real reason King Armanos had invited Camar to stay: now that his health was so bad, he was anxiously looking for a husband for his daughter. Over the coming days, the good opinion he had of Camar from the past was confirmed. In fact, he thought Camar was even kinder and gentler than before. He watched the growing friendship between him and Hayat with excitement.

Understandably, with this friendship came some relaxation on Badoura's part. Slowly, her voice returned to her own. Her stride returned to a shorter, slower one to match her companion's. And when she pushed her hair out of her face, her gestures were feminine.

One day, when they were talking and laughing together, Hayat said: 'Do you realise that my father wants us to marry?'

Badoura nearly spat her tea across the room. 'What?' she squeaked. Then, more gruffly, *'What?'*

Hayat rolled her eyes. 'You can

stop pretending. I have known for ages that you are not really Prince Camar. Will you tell me who you really are?'

Badoura told her story and explained, 'By the time I got here I was so deep in the lie that I could not tell the truth. I am sorry.'

'I understand,' said Hayat, 'but will you still marry me?'

Badoura spluttered again. 'No, of course not!'

'Why?' Hayat asked. 'I like you far more than I have ever liked any man, and my father adores you. Already he plans to give you his crown and responsibilities. He will be heartbroken if you refuse.'

'I cannot rule a kingdom I know nothing about!' cried Badoura.

'Leave it to me. I have been helping my father for years. It just does not occur to him that he could leave his crown to me instead of my husband.'

The friends shook their heads at this stupidity.

'All the same,' said Badoura, 'we cannot marry.'

'Can we at least get engaged? My father will not live to see the wedding anyway, and I want to make him happy. Please?' Then she looked at Badoura so pleadingly that Badoura could not say no.

'Very well,' she agreed.

Chapter 4

King Armanos gladly gave his permission for Prince Camar/Princess Badoura to marry his daughter. At first he urged them to have the wedding as soon as possible, but Princess Hayat insisted that all she wanted was to spend time with him while she could.

When the king's health allowed it, he and Hayat showed Badoura around the kingdom. But often there was only Hayat to explain who was who and how things were done, and she knew it all like the back of her hand. Her favourite place was the port because she liked to watch the boats come and go. Badoura did too.

'If only you had been born a man,' Badoura said, as they looked out across the glittering sea. 'You would have made an excellent king.'

Hayat shook her head. 'But I love being a woman. And I do not understand why the Isles need a king at all. Why not a queen?'

It was a very good question, but Badoura did not have the answer.

Meanwhile, on a distant shore, six months were coming to an end. It was almost time for Camar to catch the boat that would take him home. Excitement and a wish to repay the old gardener's kindness made him work harder than ever. When the old man asked him to cut down a dead tree, Camar whistled as he swung the axe.

He saw Badoura's beauty in every flower in the garden, and her sweetness in every fruit. When the desire to kiss her was overwhelming, he kissed the talisman he carried instead.

'Soon I will kiss her lips,' he said. Then he returned to swinging the axe.

CLANG.

He struck something metal. After hacking the roots away, he uncovered a bronze slab in the earth. He opened it and found some steps leading below. They led to a hand-dug cave with roots trailing from the mud roof and ten, twenty, thirty, forty, *fifty* bronze jars crowding the floor.

Camar ran back inside the cottage where the old man had been resting for days after a fall. He half carried him outside to see the discovery. He brought one jar out of the cave and reached in, letting the gold dust sift through his fingers like flour.

'Look!' he cried. 'There are fifty jars full of this. With such riches you never need to work another day in your life!'

The old man smiled weakly. 'If I never need to work another day in my life, it is because I will be dead soon.'

'Do not say that,' Camar protested.

'It is the truth, and I do not mind admitting it. I have worked this land for eighty years and only now has it given up this treasure. It was clearly meant for you to find, not I. You can take it with you when you go.'

'All I want are some olives for my wife,' Camar said. 'They are her favourite, and yours are the best I have ever tasted.'

'Take as many as you want,' said the gardener. 'You can use them to cover the gold.

'I cannot take your gold.'

'It is *your* gold, and it is safer for me if you take it. What if someone finds out about it after you are gone and tries to rob me?'

Reluctantly, Camar agreed to take half the gold and hide the rest.

At long last the boat arrived, fluttering with flags of all colours and kinds. Camar loaded the twenty-five jars aboard, each with a layer of olives at the top to hide the gold. Lastly, he added a small bag of clothes and the talisman.

'When do we sail?' he asked the captain eagerly.

'An hour,' came the answer. 'And no later.'

Camar returned to the cottage to say goodbye to the gardener and found him lying on the floor. He had fallen again. Quickly, Camar carried him to his bed and tried to make him comfortable. For a long time, the old man would not open his eyes. When he finally did, he smiled gratefully at Camar. 'Thank you,' he said.

'For what?' asked Camar. 'I am the one who should be thanking you.'

'Thank you,' the gardener

repeated, for he did not have the strength to say 'for being here with me at the end'. But he died happily because of it.

Camar wept sadly, then he ran back to the port, not to leave but to pay the captain to wait while he arranged a funeral. By the time he arrived, however, the boat was already a speck in the distance. It had sailed without him.

The boat's first stop was the port of the capital of the Black

Isles, where Badoura had taken to visiting whenever there were new arrivals. The latest boat, she learnt, carried people from all over Persia. But none of them were Camar.

'And what kind of goods do you bring to trade?' she asked to cover her disappointment.

'Everything, Your Highness,' the captain replied, for Badoura still dressed as a man. 'Fine muslin cloth, precious stones, musk, amber, medicine, spices, olives–'

'Olives?' Badoura perked up.

musk
A substance produced by certain animals that has an earthy, woodsy smell. Historically used in perfume.

'Yes, twenty-five jars of them!'

'I will take the lot,' Badoura said. 'Send them to the palace.'

The next day she and Hayat dined on salad and flatbread, with a sweet and sour side dish of plump green olives in ground walnut paste, minced garlic, chopped herbs and pomegranate juice.

'These olives are delicious,' said Hayat. 'I must give some to father.'

'There are plenty to go around,'

said Badoura. 'I bought twenty-five jars yesterday!'

Hayat laughed. 'I know you love olives, but twenty-five jars is too many even for you.'

'See for yourself.'

Badoura showed Hayat the storeroom crammed with jars. Hayat opened one and found not olives but a bag inside. She rummaged in the bag and discovered – 'A man's clothes?'

Frowning, Badoura opened another jar. All she could see inside it were olives, but as she delved deeper, her fingers met something cool and gritty like sand.

'What is this?' she asked, just as Hayat said the same thing. In Badoura's hand was gold dust. In Hayat's hand was the talisman.

Badoura gasped. 'Camar!'

From that, Hayat understood just enough to follow her friend as she raced back to the port. Badoura breathed a sigh of relief when she found the boat from Torf was still there.

'Captain,' she said. 'Where did you get those olives?'

'A young man in Torf. We had to set sail without him, but I promise I will give him the money you paid when I return.'

'When will that be?'

'Not for some time yet, Your Highness. We sail as far as the Isle of the Children of Khaledan and back again.'

'You must return there *now*!' Badoura insisted. 'I will give you twenty-five jars of gold dust to go back and bring that young man to me immediately.'

The captain's eyes grew wide at such a sum. He set off at once and the wind in his sails cut the journey time in half.

Camar was not expecting the boat to return for months, so he was not there to meet it. The captain had to track him down to the gardener's cottage, where Camar was moping.

'You must come with me to the Black Isles,' he said. 'Prince Camar wants to see you.'

'Prince Camar?' Camar was very confused by this. 'Who is he?'

'He is engaged to King Armanos's daughter.'

'Princess Hayat?'

This only confused Camar further, but the Black Isles were a step closer to home – and hopefully to Badoura – so he gladly went.

As soon as they arrived, he was taken to the palace and introduced to the prince who shared his name. Not only did the real Camar not recognise the disguised Badoura; Badoura hardly recognised Camar. His skin was brown from the sun.

His hands were rough from work. His hair was a tangled mess. And as for his clothes …

'We do not look so similar anymore,' Badoura murmured.

'What did you say, Your Highness?' asked Camar.

Badoura raised her voice and spoke as a man. 'I said you must be wondering what I brought you here for.'

'Oh, well, yes, I suppose I am, Your Highness.'

'I recently bought some olives from your captain,' Badoura explained. 'And they are far and away the best I have ever tasted. I understand that you grew them yourself. Are you a farmer?'

'Not by birth, Your Highness.'

'Then how did you come to be one now?'

'It is a very long story …'

Nevertheless, Camar told it. His host listened closely, especially when Camar explained about the bird and the talisman and the events that had kept him from his beloved wife for so long. When he described missing the boat and facing at least six more months apart, Badoura the pretend prince even cried.

'Do not be sad, Your Highness,' said Camar. 'I will be with my Badoura soon.'

'Perhaps even sooner than you think …'

Before Camar could ask what

the other man meant by this, servants came in with food and drink. There was stuffed fish and stewed meats, a mountain of rice and a riot of tangy, tart, rich and hearty flavours. And, of course, there were olives – but only a few.

They shared a small bowl between them, and talked until almost all were gone. When there was one olive left, the disguised Badoura hid it behind her back.

'Choose a hand,' she said.

The familiarity of the moment startled Camar. He remembered doing this exact thing after Badoura had appeared in his tower.

'You should eat it, Your Highness.'

'Choose a hand.'

Camar chose the left hand. It was empty. But the right one …

'My talisman!' Camar gasped.

Badoura giggled, breaking her disguise. 'I think you mean *my* talisman.'

Then she pushed back her hair and shed her thick robes, which she had used to make herself look bigger than she really was.

'Well?' she said. 'Do you not recognise your own wife?'

Camar's answer was to seize her in his arms and swing her round and round until they were both dizzy. That was how Hayat found them.

'Nice to see you again, Prince

Camar,' she said. 'I see you have met my fiancé – Prince Camar.'

'How … What …' But the real Camar could not complete a sentence.

Badoura laughed. 'It is a very long story …'

Camar agreed to continue the engagement with Hayat for the sake of her father. Slowly, carefully, Badoura returned to her life as a woman, and Camar returned to his life as a prince. They had to cover his tan with make-up – which Badoura and Hayat had lots of fun with – but no one seemed to notice the changeover. Now, whenever King Armanos spoke to Prince

Camar, he was speaking to the real one. And they spoke often before the king died.

'Look after my daughter,' Armanos said at the end. 'And listen to her advice. She knows best about the kingdom.'

'Yes, she does,' Camar agreed. 'And I promise I will look after her.'

It was the truth. After the king had passed away peacefully, Camar did not marry Hayat, but the friendship between the Prince of the Isle of the Children of Khaledan and the Queen of the Black Isles was legendary.

Camar and Badoura stayed long enough to make sure that the people of the Black Isles followed their new queen as loyally as they had followed their king. They need not have worried, for the people had always known how much Armanos relied on Hayat's help in his final years. They trusted and loved her completely.

Finally, Camar returned to his homeland and introduced his wife to his mother, father and the grand-vizier. For more than two years, King Shah Zaman had believed his son was dead.

And for more than two years, he had regretted every argument they ever had, and all the times he had kept Camar from going where and doing what he pleased.

'Forgive me,' he said.

'I do, father.'

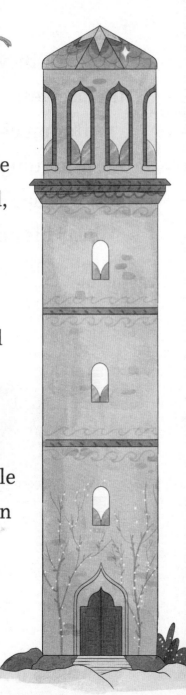

But after so much freedom, Camar did not want to live in the palace again. Instead, he had the old tower where he had met Badoura rebuilt. It became a beautiful home for them and their first child – whom everyone said was the most adorable baby ever born. When word of this reached a certain *two* genies, however, they came to judge for themselves.

After much thought – and even more arguing – even Maimoune and Danhasch had to agree.

Just this once.